© 1994 Verlag J. F. Schreiber

English translation © 1995 by Verlag J. F. Schreiber

This is a translation of *Okino und die Wale.*

Library of Congress Cataloging-in-Publication Data
Esterl, Arnica.
[Okino und die Wale. English]
Okino and the whales/written by Arnica Esterl; illustrated by Marek
Zawadzki.—1st U.S. ed.
p.   cm.
Summary: As mother waits with her son for the whales to return to the bay,
she relates a story about a girl who visited the royal palace of the whales.
ISBN 0-15-200377-0
[1. Whales—Fiction.  2. Mother and child—Fiction.  3. Japan—Fiction.]
I. Zawadzki, Marek, ill.  II. Title.
PZ7.E74860k   1995
[Fic]—dc20      94-32676

The text was set in Weiss.

A B C D E

*Printed and bound in Belgium by Proost*

ARNICA ESTERL

# OKINO
## AND THE WHALES

ILLUSTRATED BY

*Marek Zawadzki*

HARCOURT BRACE & COMPANY

*San Diego   New York   London*

Takumi, look! The whales are coming!" Okino shouted. "Can you see them spouting over there on the horizon?" she asked her son. "The whales are coming again. Isn't it wonderful!"

Okino was sitting on a flat rock, looking across the rough, gray waters of the bay. For days she had been waiting for her dark friends to return from the icy polar sea. Each year individual whales came together, forming large pods, and they hunted, mated, and gave birth in the warm, shallow waters of the bay. It seemed as if the sea itself were coming to life.

Takumi was crouched next to her. It was the first time this year that Okino had taken Takumi with her to the rock. He was now five years old and had learned to squat on his heels for hours and look across the sea with his black eyes, waiting for the whales to return, but he had never seen one.

"Can you see the whales blowing over there?" Okino asked again. Takumi strained his eyes, and yes, in the heavy swell of the sea he could now distinguish different colors. Single waves became moving dark bodies, and then suddenly one of them breached the surface and fell back into the water.

"I saw its pale stomach!" Takumi shouted with joy. "Can't I learn to swim as well as that?" he asked his mother.

"We can't swim as well as whales can, nor can we fly like birds," Okino answered.

"Whales are our swimming brothers and seagulls are our flying sisters. Shall I tell you a story about the girl who went to the royal palace of the whales, deep down at the bottom of the ocean?"

"Oh, yes!" Takumi said, and moved closer to Okino. She put her arm around his small shoulders and started to tell the story.

It happened long, long ago, when
your great-grandmother was just a
little girl. Every day she went to the
sea with her mother, who washed
other people's large, colorful
kimonos. All day long the girl
played with pebbles, seaweed, and
little sand crabs.

One day the mother had dried all
the clothes and was ready to carry
them home, when she discovered
her little girl had disappeared. The
mother looked all along the shore,
between the rocks, and in the little
tide pools. She called her daughter's
name, but there was no answer. She
asked the terns, the grasses, and the
little fishes, but none of them had
seen the girl. Finally the mother sat
down on a flat rock, tired and sad,
and looked across the sea. Had her
little girl drowned? She would not
go home without her daughter.

Then a seagull flew past and cried in a screeching voice, "Deep down at the bottom of the sea, in the crystal hall, I saw your child with a large whale."

The mother stretched her arms out longingly. "Seagull, you hover over the water all day long. Please tell me. Can I find her? Can I see her?"

The seagull shot down, picked a fish out of the water, and cried, "You must go forward, ever forward. Never stop hoping, never give up!"

The mother wept. "Won't the waves engulf me?"

The seagull was just about to fly away. But then it turned back and cried, more quietly this time, "If you carry a light in your hand, it will light you to the other land."

So the mother took her courage in both hands. She fetched a small lamp filled with fish oil, lit it, and walked into the middle of the waves. To her astonishment, she saw that her lamp continued to burn.

She walked for many hours, until she finally reached the royal palace of the whales. The seagull had spoken the truth. She entered a crystal hall that was decorated with shining mother-of-pearl, colored fins, and the most beautiful corals, and was lit by polished golden amber drops. Through a thin wall she could see children in another room, holding hands and dancing merrily. Her little daughter was there, too. She was laughing and had cheeks like ripe red apples.

The mother watched for a long time. Then she heard a deep, singsong voice. "How did you get in here and what do you want?"

She turned around to face a glittering curtain of immense whalebones hanging in front of a mouth, from which the voice had come. Behind the curtain was a huge gray figure.

"Who are you?" whispered Okino in awe.

"I am Iwa, Great Mother of the Ocean," the voice answered. Innumerable mussels and snails shimmered on her back. Sea anemones moved their long arms like dancers.

The mother stretched out her hand courageously. The little flame in the lamp burned steadily. "The light led me here. I'm looking for my child. Oh, please, Great Mother, give me back my child. Let me enter the hall!" she pleaded.

"You can't enter this hall," the deep voice rang out. "Not as long as you breathe the air of human beings. You can only see your daughter through the glass wall. But as you have had the courage to come here, I will give you a task. If you can complete it, you will free your daughter from the hall and you can take her home with you."

Iwa moved slowly toward the mother and laid herself before her like a huge breaker on the shore. Her skin shimmered with many colors, but she was cold and naked.

Once again the voice rang out. "You have carried the light into my house. I am cold. Weave a coat for me out of your own hair, so that it can warm me. Then I will give you your child back. Here is a cream, made of oil and ambergris, which will make your hair grow back quickly."

So the mother cut off all her
beautiful long black hair and started
to weave. She worked day and night,
the light burning quietly next to her.
The mussels on Iwa's back opened,
released little bubbles, and closed
again. The anemones danced their
mysterious dance. Sometimes the
mother watched, entranced, almost
forgetting her work. A long time
passed. When she had woven all
her hair, the coat was still only
half-finished. She showed it to the
Great Mother of the Ocean, but Iwa
could not be persuaded. "I must have
the whole coat," Iwa insisted.

So the mother rubbed her head with the cream and waited and waited until her hair had grown long and full again. Then she cut it off and continued to weave. At last the coat was finished. Proudly she presented it to the Great Mother Iwa. Iwa opened the door of the glass hall and led the girl, who had now grown into a young woman, out of the hall. Overjoyed, the mother embraced her daughter. Then Iwa ordered two dolphins to carry the mother and daughter back to the shore.

And so they arrived back home. But every year, when the whales and dancing dolphins played in the water and visited them, the daughter sat on a flat rock and watched. When she grew older and had children of her own, she told them all about her adventures in the palace of Iwa, the Great Mother of the Ocean. And in her hand she always carried a little burning lamp.

Okino looked down at her son. Takumi had fallen fast asleep at her side. Okino smiled and held him in her arms. Lost in thought, she watched the whales playing and waited for her son to return from the dreamworld of the Great Mother Iwa.